THIS BOOK BELONGS TO

....

For Mum and Dad. Congratulations on your 80th birthdays.
Intergalactic thanks to Susan for everything
and to Jack Lowden for reading the audio book. – AW

For Graym, my hero – CHH

Special thanks once again to Dave Gray and Paul Croan

Published by Little Door Books 2017
This edition published 2018

ISBN: 978-0-9927520-4-0

Little Door Books

mail@littledoorbooks.co.uk
www.littledoorbooks.co.uk
twitter: @littledoorbooks

ONE BUTTON BENNY

WRITTEN BY ALAN WINDRAM
ILLUSTRATED BY CHLOE HOLWILL-HUNTER

Benny was different. Benny was special.
Benny was a ROBOT.

Benny had a bright red button in the middle of his tummy.
On the button, written in big, bold letters were the words...

ONLY PRESS
IN AN
EMERGENCY

Benny had never pressed his button.
He often wondered what would happen if he did.

Benny had always known that he wasn't like the other robots. They all had lots of buttons and when they pressed them they did wonderful things.

The other robots used to tease Benny, saying:

It didn't help that Benny's mum made him wear a vest when it got cold outside.

Every time the other robots pressed their buttons they would show off, saying:

Benny often wished there was an emergency so he could press his big, red button.

One morning Benny woke up.
It seemed just like any other morning.

He had his breakfast, brushed his teeth, looked in the mirror
at his big, bright red button and wondered
what would happen if he pressed it.

But this morning there was something different...
There was something WRONG!

Outside in the street, everyone was zipping and zooming around in a panic, shouting:

Benny had heard stories about the collectors...
scary stories that kept him awake at night and
made him hide under his blanket

The collectors were

small... hairy... scary aliens with green bottoms

who travelled through space looking for bright, shiny metal. They would gather it all up, throw it into their gigantic crushing machine and turn it into teapots.

The collectors had arrived in the night when everyone was sleeping and taken over Benny's planet.

All the robots were crying as the collectors took them down the main street toward the spaceship... and their gigantic crushing machine.

Benny looked at his mum and said:

MUM, MUM,
I DON'T WANT TO BE
A TEAPOT!
WHAT ARE WE
GOING TO DO?
IS THIS AN
EMERGENCY?

YES, BENNY,
THIS IS AN
EMERGENCY.
QUICK, PRESS YOUR
BUTTON. YOU ARE
THE ONLY ONE WHO
CAN SAVE US NOW.

Benny placed his finger over the big red button on his tummy...

closed his eyes...

and pressed his button...

But nothing happened.

Then all of a sudden there was a...

then a very loud...

Benny went zooming into the sky, faster than the fastest rocket, flying higher and higher, up into space.

He pressed his button again and bright blue laser beams came shooting out of his fingers and from the toes of his boots, zapping the collectors from behind and turning their bottoms bright red.

Benny pressed his button a third time and there was a brilliant flash
of light that stretched across the whole sky.

It confused the collectors so much that they all ran around
bumping into each other.

They were so scared of Benny and what he could do that they ran as fast as they could into their spaceship...

and flew away, never to return.

All of the robots just stood and stared at Benny in amazement.

Then together they started jumping up and down, smiling and cheering and singing...

Everyone lifted Benny up on their shoulders as they sang and danced all through the town.

Later that night, Benny was still amazed at what had happened when he pressed his Big, Bright Red Button. And as his mum was tucking him up in bed, Benny asked her...

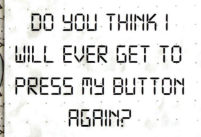

DO YOU THINK I WILL EVER GET TO PRESS MY BUTTON AGAIN?

I HOPE THAT YOU NEVER HAVE TO BENNY, BUT SOMEHOW I THINK YOU WILL.

With that, she gave Benny a goodnight kiss, turned out the light,
and before you could say Zing, Zang, Zoom...

Benny was fast asleep.

THE END.